It was a busy morning in Toy Town…

"What would I do without you, Noddy?" said Dinah Doll. "You run the best taxi service in Toy Town!"

Noddy laughed. "I run the *only* taxi service in Toy Town!"

"If there were a hundred others, I'd still choose yours," Dinah declared.

I like to drive my car, I drive it near and far.
Oh, I'm the best by far. Yes, I'm a taxi star.
Noddy sang as he polished a speck of dust
off his car. Then he heard the Toy Town clock.
"Noon! Time to pick up Mr Wobbly Man."

Noddy was driving into the square, when all of a sudden, a strange bicycle taxi trundled to a halt ahead of him. It belonged to Sly and Gobbo, the two bad goblins.

"Oh, no!" gasped Noddy, as Mr Wobbly Man rolled into the strange taxi.

"You're not the only taxi in Toy Town now," sneered Gobbo.

Mr Wobbly Man leaned out of the goblins' taxi. "I'm sorry, Noddy, but the goblins were here first. And they're giving me a free ride!"

"That's all right, Mr Wobbly Man," called Noddy. "Enjoy your ride!"

Big-Ears arrived as Noddy was puzzling over why the goblins would want to give free rides.

"Did you see that strange-looking bicycle taxi?" Noddy asked him.

"Yes," replied Big-Ears. "Those goblins are up to something."

"I don't think so," said Noddy. "They just want to give taxi rides, like I do."

Big-Ears was still not happy. "You watch out for those goblins, Noddy."

"I will," replied Noddy, "but I'm sure there's nothing to worry about."

Noddy drove on through Toy Town.

"Ah, there's Mrs Skittle. She wants me to give her a lift," he cried.

But before he could stop, Sly and Gobbo screeched up in front of him.

"Need a lift, lady?" yelled Gobbo. Mrs Skittle hesitated.

"It's free!" he cooed. How could she possibly say no?

"Hey! That's twice today you've stolen my passengers!" Noddy shouted at the two chortling goblins.

"You may be cheaper but I'm better!" Noddy boasted. "My little car can take passengers faster than you ever could in that bicycle thing."

"Noddy's right," said Mrs Skittle as she jumped out of the goblins' bicycle taxi and into Noddy's car.
"The goblins' ride may be free," she said, "but I need to get to Mr Straw's farm fast."
PARP! PARP! Noddy beeped his horn and grinned at the scowling goblins as he drove off.

"Our free rides were meant to stop people using Noddy's taxi service," moaned Gobbo, "so we would be the only taxi in Toy Town. And then we could charge *three* times as much!"

"It was a brilliant idea," groaned Sly. "But it won't work. Noddy's taxi will always be faster."

"We have to think of another plan," said Gobbo.

"That'll be hard," sighed Sly. "Noddy has a car and we don't."

Gobbo's eyes lit up. "That's it! We get rid of Noddy's car! Then we'll really be the only taxi service in Toy Town."

Late that night the two goblins were creeping towards Noddy's garage.

"Hurry! Get the door open quick, before someone spots us!" whispered Gobbo.

Sly and Gobbo could just see Noddy's shiny car in the gloom of the garage.

"Now!" hissed Gobbo, as he threw a small bag at the engine. Whoosh! A powdery cloud showered down on Noddy's car.

"Noddy's going to get a big surprise," they sniggered as they slipped away.

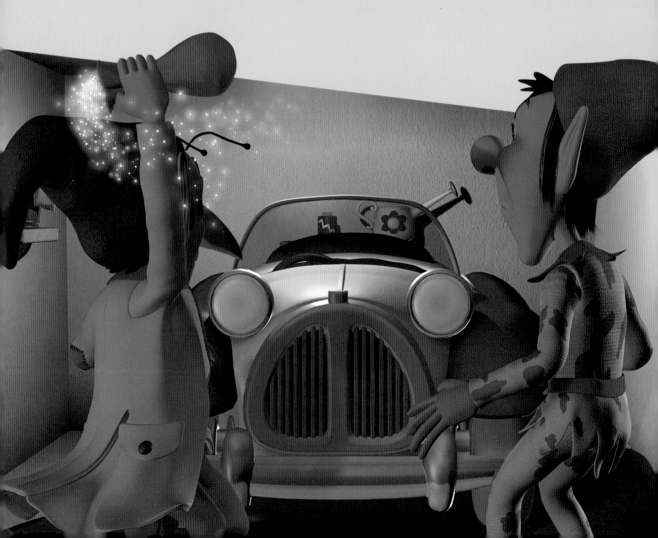

Next morning, Noddy jumped into his car
and drove off, eager to start work.

SCREECH! The car suddenly lurched to a halt,
whirled around, and zoomed off again.

"Help!" yelped Noddy. The car seemed to have
a mind of its own! He couldn't stop it!

No matter how hard Noddy tried, the car would
not drive straight. It drove in crazy circles,
knocked over lamp posts, crashed against
benches, and frightened everyone.

"HALT!" ordered Mr Plod, stepping into the
road. But the car drove straight at him…

Just in the nick of time, SCREECH! the car came
to a sudden stop.

Mr Plod was very angry.

"Noddy, that was very dangerous!" he shouted.

"But it wasn't me, it was the car!" Noddy cried.

"I tried to stop, but I couldn't," said Noddy.
"Honestly, Mr Plod!"

"Hmm," said Mr Plod. "But I'm still taking
you and your car to jail. It'll be a long time
before you give anyone else a taxi ride!"

"This is the only taxi in Toy Town. Who wants a ride?" shouted Sly and Gobbo.

With Noddy and his car locked up, they were putting their plan into action. They skidded to a halt next to Mrs Skittle.

"Where to, lady?" asked Gobbo.

"Home, please," said Mrs Skittle.

"That'll be six coins, please," Gobbo demanded.

"Six!" Mrs Skittle was shocked. "Noddy only charges two!"

"Well, Noddy's in jail," Gobbo sneered. "So, if you want a ride, we're it. Cough up the coins, lady."

Mrs Skittle had to pay the goblins what they wanted.

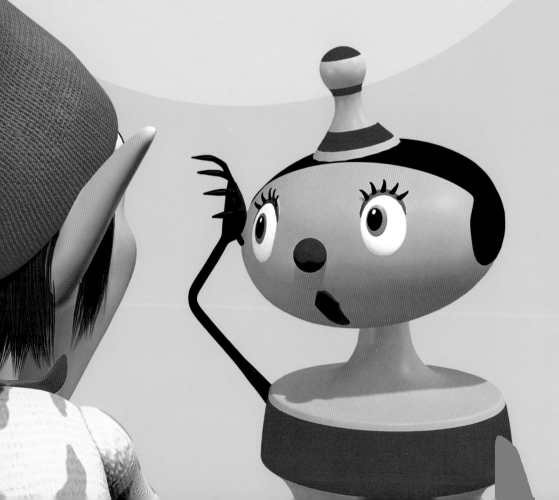

"But it wasn't me," wailed Noddy to Big-Ears who had hurried round to the jail. "It was the car! It went crazy. I couldn't stop it. Truly!"

Mr Plod frowned. "But Mr Sparks has looked at the car and there's nothing wrong with it."

"Perhaps," said Big-Ears, "it's a *different* sort of problem."

Noddy and Mr Plod looked puzzled.

Big-Ears took a long sniff at Noddy's car. "Ah ha! Just as I guessed! Someone's put a magic spell on it!" he cried.

"It's a silly spell," explained Big-Ears. "It makes things act in a crazy way."

"Can you get rid of it?" Noddy asked.

"No," said Big-Ears. "Only the person who made the spell can take it off. Now, Noddy, who would want you out of the way?" Big-Ears asked.

Noddy thought for a moment.

"Sly and Gobbo! With me out of the way, they'd have the only taxi in Toy Town!" said Noddy.

"You may be right, Noddy!" said Big-Ears. "Let's see." He sprinkled a fine dust over the car, chanting:

Leaf of oak and foxglove seed
Hazelnut and blade of grass
Make the culprits of this deed
Appear before us at high speed.

"Hey! What's happening?" yelped the two goblins as an invisible force dragged them backwards towards the police station.

"Pedal, Sly. Pedal!" shouted Gobbo.

They both pedalled like mad, but Big-Ears' magic was too strong!

"Here they come!" said Big-Ears, as the goblins whizzed across the road and crashed into the police station.

"Ooh!" gasped the goblins, tumbling out of the wreck.

Mr Plod grabbed each of them, at once.

"Don't tell him anything, Sly," warned Gobbo.

"Don't worry, I won't tell them we put a spell on Noddy's ca… Oops!" Sly clamped a hand over his mouth, but it was too late.

"I knew it!" Mr Plod exploded. "Now, you bad goblins, take that spell off, at once!" he barked.

The goblins had to do what they were told.

"You're Toy Town's only taxi service again, Noddy," said Big-Ears smiling.

"Yes! And I'll always be the best," grinned Noddy, as he drove off to pick up his next passenger.

I like to drive my car, I drive it near and far.

*The horn is sharp, it goes **parp-parp**!*

And I'm the best by far. Yes, I'm a taxi star.

This edition published 2004 for Index Books Limited

First published in Great Britain by HarperCollins Publishers Ltd in 2002

1 3 5 7 9 10 8 6 4 2

ISBN: 0 00 770121 7

Printed and bound in China